WHEN MONTY MET ALFIE

By Maggie Holden

CW00703865

MAPLE
PUBLISHERS

When Monty Met Alfie

Author: Maggie Holden

Illustrations by Denis Stapleton

Copyright © Maggie Holden (2022)

The right of Maggie Holden to be identified as author of this work has been asserted by the author in accordance with section 77 and 78 of the Copyright, Designs and Patents Act 1988.

First Published in 2022

ISBN 978-1-915164-43-8 (Paperback)

Published by:
    Maple Publishers
    1 Brunel Way,
    Slough,
    SL1 1FQ, UK
    www.maplepublishers.com

Book Layout by:
    White Magic Studios
    www.whitemagicstudios.co.uk

A CIP catalogue record for this title is available from the British Library.

All rights reserved. No part of this book may be reproduced or translated by any form or by any means, electronic or mechanical, including photocopying, recording or by any information storage and retrieval system without written permission from the author.

The views expressed in this work are solely those of the author and do not necessarily reflect the views of the publisher, and the publisher hereby disclaims any responsibility for them.

*In loving memory of Monty who was
the inspiration for this book.*

Alfie still lives next door.

Monty loved his garden.
He'd be in it all day long,
Playing, sleeping, watching,
While the blackbird sang his song.

His garden was on the river bank
Where gentle waters ran
And ducks would quack and make a noise
As loudly as they can.

His favourite place was a wooden bench
Right near the water's edge,
Where he could watch the river
And see his neighbour's hedge.

To him it was a great surprise
When through the hedge one day
A friendly ginger kitten came
To ask if he would play.

When Monty Met Alfie

"Play," roared Monty, "I'm too old for that,
But there's lots I've got to tell.
So first things first –who are you ?
I need to know you well."

"I'm Alfie," said the little cat.
"I'm only four months old.
I live in the house next door to you
And I'm learning to be bold."

"No problem there," said Monty.
"I can teach you a thing or two.
I've sixteen years experience
Of everything cats can do."

So Alfie lay down on the seat
And they dozed in the summer sun.
"When nighttime comes," said Monty,
"That's when we'll have our fun."

They chatted and dozed, went home to eat
Waiting for nighttime to fall.
When the moon popped up and the stars shone out
They heard the barn owl's call.

"What's that ?" cried Alfie holding his ears.

"That's a very eerie sound".

"Nothing to fear," replied Monty

"Only the barn owl flying round."

"Follow me now," said Monty
"Let's go down to the potting shed.
There's lots of mice beneath the floor
And my tummy can be fed."

They hunted under the potting shed.
They foraged in the grass.
They chased and laughed, enjoyed themselves,
'Til daybreak came to pass.

Then weary cats went to their homes
To wash from tail to head.
To feed themselves, until tummies full
They climbed upstairs to bed.

So Monty and Alfie became good friends
And daily Alfie grew
And through the days and through the nights
Monty taught him all he knew.

Alfie learned about the ducks and the long
necked swan,
About the squirrel scampering by,
The moles and voles, the frogs and toads,
And the inhabitants of the sky.

He followed Monty up the trees.

They sat upon the shed.

He followed Monty to the river

And everywhere Monty led.

They clawed their way up the trellis
And onto the garden wall.
They clambered onto the outhouse roof
Never afraid that they would fall.

They slept upon the summerhouse roof.
They slept inside the trug.
They slept inside the arbour
And on the backdoor rug.

They slept in the garden under the tree.

They slept on their favourite seat.

They slept under the bushes

Away from the summer heat.

But always in the night they prowled,
In gardens far and wide,
Monty the expert hunter,
With Alfie by his side.

By the time that winter had taken hold
And the swallows had flown away,
Alfie went out on his own,
Stayed up all night and slept all day.

Sometimes he joined Monty on the bench
In the warmth of a springtime day
And occasionally he would ask him
"Do you remember when I wanted to play ?"

"I'll never forget, " said Monty,
Sitting in the sun,
"How a tiny little ginger cat
Has given me so much fun."

It was with a sigh that ageing Monty slept
Contentedly in the sun
And Alfie cat went on his way.
His new adventures had begun.

CPSIA information can be obtained
at www.ICGtesting.com
Printed in the USA
LVHW071619240122
709246LV00007B/286